MARY HOFFMAN has written more than 70 books for children and in 1998 was made an Honorary Fellow of the Library Association for services to children's library issues. She is also the editor of a quarterly children's book review called Armadillo. Her book *Song of the Earth* (Orion) was shortlisted for the Kurt Maschler Award in 1995. In 1992 *Amazing Grace*, her first book for Frances Lincoln, was selected for Child Education's Best Books of 1991 and Children's Books of the Year 1992, commended for the Kate Greenaway Medal, and included on the National Curriculum Reading List in 1996 and 1997. Its sequel, *Grace & Family*, was among Junior Education's Best Books of 1995 and shortlisted for the Sheffield Libraries Book Award 1996. It was followed by *An Angel Just Like Me*, *A Twist in the Tail*, *Three Wise Women* and *Women of Camelot*. Her first Bible story collaboration with Jackie Morris was on *Parables: Stories Jesus Told*.

JACKIE MORRIS grew up in the Cotswolds and studied illustration at Bath Academy. She has worked in magazine publishing and designed greetings cards for Greenpeace, Amnesty International and Oxfam, and her paintings have been exhibited in Bath, London, and throughout Australia. *Lord of the Dance* (Lion), *Grandmother's Song* and *Susan Summers' The Greatest Gift* (both Barefoot), Anita Ganeri's *Journeys Through Dreamtime* (Macdonald Young Books) and Ted Hughes' *How the Whale Became* (Faber) are some of her most recent books. Her first two collaborations with Caroline Pitcher for Frances Lincoln were on *The Snow Whale* and *The Time of the Lion* – about which Books for Keeps commented, "There is a strength and majesty in the watercolour illustrations which flow across the gutter of the book on every page." They were followed by *Mariana and the Merchild*, also written by Caroline Pitcher, and *Parables: Stories Jesus Told*.

For Luke Sorby, Kerry and Paul's own miracle
— M.H.

 For Catherine and Sam, with much love
— J.M.

Miracles: Wonder Jesus Worked
Copyright @ Frances Lincoln Limited 2001
Text copyright @ Mary Hoffman 2001
Illustrations copyright @ Jackie Morris 2001

First published in Great Britain in 2001 by
Frances Lincoln Limited, 4 Torriano Mews
Torriano Avenue, London NW5 2RZ

First paperback edition 2002

British Library Cataloguing in Publication Data
available on request

ISBN 0-7112-1569-3 hardback
ISBN 0-7112-1814-5 paperback

Set in Meridien

Printed in Singapore
1 3 5 7 9 8 6 4 2

MARY HOFFMAN ◆ JACKIE MORRIS

MIRACLES

◆ WONDERS JESUS WORKED ◆

FRANCES LINCOLN

CONTENTS

What is a miracle? It looks a lot like magic. For a miracle to happen, at least one of the laws of nature has to be overturned. Jesus could walk on water, cure people without even meeting them, feed thousands with a few odds and ends, and control the weather. And in the greatest miracle of all, he brought someone who had died back to life.

Christians believe that Jesus was both human and God – so he could do anything. But he didn't do anything to save himself from his own cruel death. That is in some ways more marvellous than any miracle.

The stories of Jesus' miracles are some of the most famous in the Bible – the feeding of the five thousand, the bulging net of fishes, stilling the storm. I have chosen nine of them, ranging from what John tells us was Jesus' first miracle – turning water into wine – to the raising of his good friend Lazarus from the dead.

And it was the last miracle which sealed Jesus' fate. No one who was rumoured to have such power over life and death could be allowed to live.

Mary Hoffman

WATER into WINE

Have you ever been to a wedding? In Jesus' time, just like today, it was a reason to give a really big party for all the family and friends of the young couple getting married. But can you imagine what it would be like if all the nice things to drink ran out – all the lemonade and the orange-juice, and the wine and beer for the grown-ups – and there was nothing left but water?

Some friends of Jesus' mother, Mary, were being married at a place called Cana, in Galilee. We don't know their names for sure, but some people think the bridegroom was Jesus' close friend John, who later became his favourite disciple and wrote one of the four Gospels. Anyway, the couple must have known Mary very well, because they invited not only Jesus, but his friends who became the disciples.

Maybe they invited too many people. Whatever the reason, the party ran out of wine. When Jesus and his friends arrived, they asked for something to drink, and Mary said, "They have no wine."

Jesus knew that she meant him to do something about it and he said rudely, "What do you expect of me? The time isn't right."

"Do whatever he tells you," Mary said to the servants. She understood her son very well and guessed that he was going to do something marvellous.

There were some huge stone pots for water standing in the room and Jesus told the servants to fill them to the brim. Then he told them to pour out some of the water and take it to the master-of-ceremonies of the wedding-feast.

And when the master-of-ceremonies tasted the water, it had become wine! He sent for the bridegroom and said to him, "Most people serve their best wine first and leave their cheaper wine to serve at the end, when no one can tell the difference. But you have kept your best wine until last."

How puzzled the bridegroom must have been! But the servants knew that the "best wine" had been ordinary water a few minutes before. And Jesus' disciples knew who had turned the water into wine.

This was Jesus' first miracle. It wasn't dramatic: not many people heard about it. But it made his disciples sure that Jesus was no ordinary man.

A NETFUL of FISH

Have you ever tried to catch a fish? It's not that easy. Whether you use a rod or a net, fish are very quick and slippery. Jesus had many friends who caught fish for a living. When they caught a lot, they sold them for good money. But on some days they couldn't catch any.

When Jesus first began to tell people about God, crowds gathered to hear him. So Jesus asked his friend Simon Peter, who was a fisherman, if he could use his boat. He got into the boat and Simon Peter took it out a little way from the shore. Everyone settled down on the bank, while Jesus sat in the boat and told them the good news about God's love.

When he had finished, he said to Simon Peter, "Launch out further into the lake and let down your nets."

Simon said, "Master, we have been trying to catch fish all night. There are none to be had. But if you want, I shall let down the nets."

So he did – and straight away he felt the nets straining. He could scarcely haul them on board, because they were filled to the brim with shoals of silvery fishes. There were so many that Simon Peter's nets couldn't hold them and they broke, spilling lots of fish back into the sea.

Simon Peter called out to his friends, James and John, who were also out fishing on the lake. "Come and help! There are enough fish for all of us!"

That night, they caught so many fish that both boats were full and in danger of sinking under the load.

When he saw the amazing quantities of fish, Simon Peter was ashamed that he had doubted Jesus' advice and said, "I am not worthy to follow you."

Jesus just laughed, and said, "From now on, my friend, it will be people you catch, not fish."

WEATHERMASTER

Have you ever been caught in a really bad thunderstorm? It can be terrifying. Lots of people are scared of thunder and lightning, even when they are grown up. But imagine how much worse it would be if you were in a little boat on the open sea.

Many of Jesus' friends were fishermen and he often travelled in their fishing boats. One day, when he was tired after preaching to large crowds, he asked some friends to take him and his disciples in their ship to the other side of the lake known as the Sea of Galilee.

As soon as he came on board the ship, Jesus went into the stern, where he settled down on a pillow and fell deeply asleep.

But while Jesus slept, a storm blew up over the water. Big black clouds swept over the sky and big, heavy drops of rain fell on the deck, but Jesus slept on. The wind whipped the water into huge waves, and the little boat was tossed up and down and from side to side. The waves smashed down over the sides of the ship so that it filled with water. But still Jesus slept.

The disciples were terrified. They had never known a storm like it. They frantically baled out water from the bottom of the ship. But it was no good: the boat was sinking.

"We're going to drown!" cried one. "Quick, wake up Jesus! He's the only one who can save us!"

Jesus woke, refreshed, and looked at his rain-soaked

and trembling friends. He shook his head. "How little faith you have!" he said.

Then he stood up in the boat and raised his arms. He spoke sternly to the storm, but the disciples couldn't hear his words for the howling of the wind and the driving rain. Immediately the wind dropped, the rain stopped and the water became as calm as a mill-pond.

The men on board the ship were even more frightened by the calm than by the storm.

"What kind of man is this," they asked, "if even the winds and waves obey him?"

◆ THROUGH the ROOF ◆

Have you ever wished that you could make someone better?
If you have a friend, or someone in your family who is very ill,
you want them to be cured as soon as possible. When the
word got around that Jesus could perform miracles,
all the people who were ill came to look for him.

Jesus was with his disciples in a house in Capernaum when word got around that he was there. First, one or two sick people came to ask him to make them better. Then more and more came to the house, and soon there were crowds clamouring to get in.

The sitting-room was full to overflowing and people spilled out on to the street. And still more sick people kept coming, in the hope that this miracle-worker could cure them. There were some doctors of law in the neighbourhood who were watching what was going on.

Four men came along, carrying a friend of theirs on a makeshift bed. Now, this friend had been paralysed for a long time and couldn't walk. He was full of hope that Jesus could make him better.

But when the four friends reached the house with their burden, they saw that there was no chance of getting in.

"What shall we do?" said one.

"We can't go back without seeing Jesus – we've come so far," said another.

"Let's try the roof!" said a third.

So the four friends climbed, with great difficulty, up on to the roof of the house where Jesus was, carrying

the bed between them and trying not to hurt their sick friend. When they got to the top, they made a hole in the roof. Then they lowered their friend very gently through the hole.

Imagine the surprise of Jesus and his disciples when they saw a bed descending from the ceiling, with a helpless man in it!

Jesus realised straight away how great these people's faith in him was. He went to the paralysed man and said, "Your sins are forgiven."

Everyone was very surprised, especially the doctors of law, who were listening carefully. They had expected him to say something like, "You are better now." Jesus knew this. He said to them, "Which do you think is easier to say: 'Yours sins are forgiven', or, 'Take up your bed and walk'?"

No one answered. Jesus said, "The son of man can do both."

Then he turned to the sick man and said, "Get up, pick up your bed and walk out of here on your own."

And the paralysed man rose to his feet, picked up his bed and walked steadily to the door. His friends peered down through the hole in the roof in amazement.

But the doctors of law muttered to one another, "Who does he think he is? Only God can forgive sins."

These were powerful men, and their disapproval meant danger for Jesus.

THE BIGGEST PICNIC
in the WORLD

Have you ever been in a really big crowd of people? Today, whenever large numbers of people gather together in a theme park or at a music festival, there are lots of vans and stalls and cafés selling fast food. But by the shores of Lake Galilee there was nothing but rocks and grass.

The more Jesus spoke to the people, the more people turned up to hear him. He spoke like no other preacher they had ever heard. He told them that God loved them and would forgive them their sins. And he healed people who had been blind or deaf or unable to walk since they were born.

Soon, wherever Jesus went, a huge crowd of people began to follow him. He was talking to such a crowd one hot and dusty day. When he finished speaking, one of his disciples came to him and said, "Lord, we should tell the people to go away now, so that they can buy food in the nearby villages."

But Jesus said, "Why don't we feed them here?"

Now, the disciples had counted and knew there were about five thousand people sitting on the ground, waiting to see what Jesus would do next. They went among them to see if anyone had brought any food.

And there was one boy who had a basket with his lunch in it. There were five small loaves, not much bigger than a roll, and two little cooked fish.

"This is all the food there is, Lord," said the disciples. Jesus took up the basket and blessed the food, giving thanks to God for it.

"Take the basket and feed all the people," he said.

"All the people?" thought the disciples. "There's hardly enough here to feed one!"

Still, the disciples did as they were told and took the basket to the first row of people. And all the people ate as much as they wanted – and yet there was still enough in the basket to feed the next row, and the next.

And so it went on, until all five thousand people had eaten well from five small loaves and two little fishes. And at the end there was still enough food left to fill twelve baskets!

IS IT A GHOST?

Some of the miracles that Jesus did, like healing illnesses, can now be done by science and medicine. We may feel that there is no more need for miracles. After all, people have even walked on the moon. But no one has yet walked on water – and that's exactly what Jesus did.

After Jesus had fed the crowds on the shores of Galilee, he was afraid that the people would force him to become their king. And that was not what he wanted. So he went away up the mountainside by himself to pray, and the disciples went on board a ship and waited for him on the lake.

And in the middle of the night, they saw someone walking across the water towards the ship, in the dark. They were terrified. "Is it a ghost?" they asked.

But Jesus called to them, "Don't be afraid. It's me, Jesus."

And Peter said, "Is it really you? Call me to come to you across the water."

"Come," said Jesus.

So Peter stepped off the side of the ship and started to walk to Jesus across the lake. The disciples hung over the side of the ship, open-mouthed at the sight of an ordinary man like them – their old friend Peter – acting like Jesus and doing the impossible.

Peter was just as surprised as they were. Imagine what it must have felt like: skimming over the water, breaking all the laws of nature. But after a few steps, Peter looked down and saw the deep waters of Galilee under his feet. He became afraid, and as soon as he was afraid he started to sink.

"Help! Save me, Lord!" he cried.

And Jesus took him by the hand and led him across the waves and safely back on to the ship.

"You shouldn't have been afraid," he said.

And the disciples fell at Jesus' feet and worshipped him.

"You really are the son of God," they said.

REMOTE CONTROL

*We are used to doing things at a distance. We can contact people
in other countries by phone, e-mail and the Internet. But at the time
when Jesus lived, there were no such devices – in fact, they would have
seemed like miracles themselves. In this story, what struck people
as miraculous was not the healing of an illness, but the fact
that Jesus wasn't even there when it happened.*

At the time of Jesus, the Romans were in charge in Israel. They had a governor and an army stationed there.

There was a high-ranking Roman soldier in Capernaum whose favourite servant was ill and close to death. He had heard about Jesus and was absolutely sure that this Jewish healer could make his servant better. But he also knew that it might cause trouble if Jesus was seen entering a Roman soldier's house.

He sent a message to Jesus, telling him his problem. Some friends came to Jesus and said, "You should help this Roman. He is a good man and he has been kind to us Jews."

So Jesus set out towards the soldier's house. But before Jesus reached him, the soldier sent another message, saying, "There is no need for you to come to my house. I know what it is to give orders and to be obeyed. If I tell a man to do something, he does it. All you need to do is say that my servant will get better, and I know he will."

Jesus was amazed. He said to his followers, "This Roman has more faith than any of my fellow-Jews. He believes I can heal his servant without even seeing or touching him."

And when the soldier's messenger got back to the house, he found that the servant who had been on the verge of death was sitting up in bed, looking perfectly well again.

Jesus had cured him from a distance, just as the Roman soldier had believed he would.

BACK from the DEAD

Have you ever known anyone who died? Death is so final that we find it very difficult to come to terms with. We wish that the dead person could be brought back to life. Jesus' last miracle involving another person made that wish a reality.

By now, Jesus had performed so many miracles that everyone was talking about him. Many of the Jews didn't like people believing that Jesus was the son of God. They thought it would cause trouble with the Romans. And the Romans thought Jesus was a dangerous man.

So Jesus kept well out of the way of people in power, because he knew they would use the smallest excuse to have him arrested and put to death. He and his disciples left Judaea and crossed over the river Jordan.

But while they were there, Jesus heard some bad news. He was great friends with a man called Lazarus and his two sisters, Martha and Mary. The women sent Jesus a message that Lazarus was very ill.

Jesus waited two days, then said to the disciples, "Let's go back to Judaea."

"It isn't safe, Lord," said the disciples. "You will be killed if you return there."

"My friend Lazarus is asleep," said Jesus.

"Well, if he's only asleep, you needn't go to him," said the disciples.

"I mean that Lazarus is dead," said Jesus. "And I'm glad we weren't there, because now I can really teach you to believe."

Then the disciples agreed to go back with him, even though they all believed that they might be in danger for being Jesus' friends.

When they got to Lazarus' house in Bethany, near Jerusalem, they found that the dead man had been in his tomb for four days.

Martha came out to greet Jesus, but Mary stayed in the house. Martha said, "If you had been here, my brother would not have died." And then she said, "Even now, if you ask God, I think he will do what you ask."

Jesus said, "Do you believe that I am the son of God?" And Martha replied, "Yes, Lord."

Then she ran and found her sister Mary and they both went with Jesus to Lazarus' tomb. On the way, Jesus wept for the death of his friend.

The tomb was a cave with a big rock rolled in front to make a door. Jesus told his disciples to roll the stone away.

Martha said, "Lord, our brother has been dead four days – his body will stink."

And Jesus said, "If you believe, you will see the glory of God." Then he prayed to God and called in a loud voice, "Come out, Lazarus!"

And Lazarus, who had been dead, stepped out of the cave, still wrapped in his grave clothes. Jesus had performed his greatest miracle.

But from then on the rumours spread, and it was only a few weeks before Jesus was arrested and put to death. And three days later, he too rose from the grave and visited his disciples again. It is this central miracle of Jesus' life which makes Christians believe him to be the son of God.

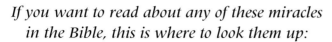 # ABOUT the STORIES

*If you want to read about any of these miracles
in the Bible, this is where to look them up:*

WATER INTO WINE *(The marriage at Cana)*

This is found only in John 2, 1-11. John makes a point of saying
that it was the first miracle of Jesus' ministry.

A NETFUL OF FISH *(The miraculous draught of fishes)*

Luke 5. 1-11. In John 21, 1-14 the miracle takes place after
the Resurrection.

WEATHERMASTER *(Stilling the storm)*

Matthew 8. 23-27; Luke 8. 22-25; Mark 4. 35-41.

THROUGH THE ROOF *(The man cured of palsy)*

Mark 2, 1-12; Luke 5, 18-26

THE BIGGEST PICNIC IN THE WORLD
(Feeding the five thousand)

This miracle can be found in all four gospels. In Matthew
and Mark, it takes place just after the death of John the Baptist.
There are similar accounts of Jesus feeding four thousand people
in Matthew 14, 15-21; Mark 6, 32-44; Luke 9, 12-17; and John 6,
5-14.

IS IT A GHOST? *(Walking on the water)*

Mark 6, 45-52; Matthew 14, 22-33; John 6, 15-21.

REMOTE CONTROL *(The centurion's servant)*

Matthew 8, 5-13; Luke 7, 2-10.

SAYING THANK YOU *(The ten lepers)*

Luke 17, 11-19.

BACK FROM THE DEAD *(The raising of Lazarus)*

Jesus also raised Jairus' daughter and at least one other person
from the dead. But John makes it very clear how this final miracle
led to Jesus' own death, in John 11, 1-46.

OTHER PICTURE BOOKS IN PAPERBACK
FROM FRANCES LINCOLN

PARABLES: STORIES JESUS TOLD

Mary Hoffman

Illustrated by Jackie Morris

In eight spirited retellings, Mary Hoffman shows how Jesus used simple storytelling
to explain God's idea of truth, fairness and love. Jackie Morris's atmospheric illustrations
bring alive the power of the parables 2,000 years after they were first told.

Suitable for National Curriculum English – Reading, Key Stage 2; and for Religious Education, Key Stages 2 and 3
Scottish Guidelines English Language – Reading, Level B; Religious and Moral Education, Levels C and D

ISBN 0-7112-1468-9 £5.99

AN ANGEL JUST LIKE ME

Mary Hoffman

Illustrated by Cornelius Van Wright and Ying-Hwa Hu

When Tyler picks up a broken Christmas-tree angel, he asks,
"Why are they always pink? Aren't there any black angels?"
It's a question no one can answer – until Tyler tells his friend Carl the problem.

"This is a beautiful book, with a story that makes you smile
and think at the same time."
Trevor Phillips

Suitable for National Curriculum English – Reading, Key Stages 1 and 2
Scottish Guidelines English Language – Reading, Levels A and B

ISBN 0-7112-1309-7 £5.99

MARIANA AND THE MERCHILD

Caroline Pitcher

Illustrated by Jackie Morris

One day, old Mariana finds a Merbaby inside a crab shell, and at once
she loves it more than life itself – although she knows that one day the
Merchild's mother will come to take her daughter back …
An enchanting folk tale set on the shores of Chile.

Suitable for National Curriculum English – Reading, Key Stages 1 and 2
Scottish Guidelines English Language Reading – Levels B and C

ISBN 0-7112-1464-6 £5.99

Frances Lincoln titles are available from all good bookshops.
Prices are correct at time of publication, but may be subject to change.